Dear Parent:

Congratulations! Your child is taking the first steps on an exciting journey. The destination? Independent reading!

STEP INTO READING® will help your child get there. The program offers five steps to reading success. Each step includes fun stories and colorful art. There are also Step into Reading Sticker Books, Step into Reading Math Readers, Step into Reading Write-In Readers, Step into Reading Phonics Readers, and Step into Reading Phonics First Steps! Boxed Sets—a complete literacy program with something for every child.

Learning to Read, Step by Step!

Ready to Read   Preschool–Kindergarten
• big type and easy words • rhyme and rhythm • picture clues
For children who know the alphabet and are eager to begin reading.

Reading with Help   Preschool–Grade 1
• basic vocabulary • short sentences • simple stories
For children who recognize familiar words and sound out new words with help.

Reading on Your Own   Grades 1–3
• engaging characters • easy-to-follow plots • popular topics
For children who are ready to read on their own.

Reading Paragraphs   Grades 2–3
• challenging vocabulary • short paragraphs • exciting stories
For newly independent readers who read simple sentences with confidence.

Ready for Chapters   Grades 2–4
• chapters • longer paragraphs • full-color art
For children who want to take the plunge into chapter books but still like colorful pictures.

STEP INTO READING® is designed to give every child a successful reading experience. The grade levels are only guides. Children can progress through the steps at their own speed, developing confidence in their reading, no matter what their grade.

Remember, a lifetime love of reading starts with a single step!

For Ramona and Leo

Visit us on the Web!
www.stepintoreading.com
www.randomhouse.com/kids/disney

Educators and librarians, for a variety of teaching tools, visit us at
www.randomhouse.com/teachers

Library of Congress Cataloging-in-Publication Data
Jordan, Apple.
A fairy tale / by Apple Jordan.
    p. cm. — (Step into reading. Step 3)
Summary: Not so sure that she wants to be a tinker fairy, Tinker Bell asks
her friends to help her find a new talent—with disastrous results.
ISBN 978-0-7364-2475-2 (trade pbk.) — ISBN 978-0-7364-8055-0 (lib. bdg.)
[1. Fairies—Fiction. 2. Self-acceptance—Fiction.] I. Title.
PZ7.J755Fa 2008
[E]—dc22
2008007565

Printed in the United States of America   18 17 16   First Edition

A Fairy Tale

By Apple Jordan
Illustrated by the Disney Storybook Artists

Random House New York

It was a special day

in Pixie Hollow.

All the fairies gathered around.

With a sprinkling of pixie dust,

a new fairy was born.

Her name was Tinker Bell.

Queen Clarion welcomed
the newest fairy.
"Born of laughter.
Clothed in cheer.
Happiness
has brought you here."

The fairies tried to help

Tinker Bell find her talent.

They gave her

flowers, water, and light.

But everything Tink

touched faded away.

Then Tinker Bell
passed a hammer.
It began to glow.
It flew straight toward her.
She had found her talent.
She was a tinker fairy.

The tinker fairies came
to welcome Tinker Bell.
Tink was happy to meet them.
She was also a bit sad.
Tinkers weren't fancy
like the other fairies.

Tink's new friends,

Clank and Bobble,

took her on a tour

of Pixie Hollow.

They saw all the fairies

getting ready for spring.

"It's the changing of the seasons!"

explained Bobble.

There was a lot going on
at Tinkers' Nook.
Tinker Bell loved seeing
all the useful things
the tinker fairies made.

Fairy Mary was the head tinker.
She told Clank and Bobble
to deliver their creations
to the rest of the fairies fast.
They would need the items
on the mainland.
"The mainland sounds
flitterific!" cried Tink.

The tinker fairies
showed the queen
what they had made.
One of Tinker Bell's creations
still needed some work.
Tink would fix it in time
to take it with her
to the mainland.

The queen told Tink that
tinker fairies did not go
to the mainland.
"Your work is here
in Pixie Hollow,"
Queen Clarion said.

"Being a tinker stinks,"
said Tinker Bell
back at Tinkers' Nook.
Fairy Mary told her that
she should be proud
of who she was.

But Tinker Bell did not
want to be a tinker.
She wanted to be a nature fairy.
She asked her friends
for help.

First Silvermist

tried to teach Tink

how to be a water fairy.

But Tink was not good

with water.

Then Iridessa tried to teach
Tink how to be a light fairy.
But Tink was not good
with light.

Fawn tried to show Tink
how to be an animal fairy.
But Tink was not good
with animals, either.

Tink saw a
big bird flying in the sky.
"Maybe that guy can help,"
she said.
The bird made a
nosedive for Tink.
"Hawk!" yelled the fairies
as they ran for cover.

Tink jumped into a hole to hide.

The hole was Vidia's hiding spot.

Now the hawk

was after Vidia, too.

The other fairies

attacked the hawk with berries.

Vidia was safe.

But she was angry.

Tink tried to help her clean up,

but she didn't want Tink's help.

Tink felt horrible.

She couldn't hold drops of water.

She couldn't hold rays of light.

Baby birds were afraid of her.

"I'm useless," she said.

Tink flew to the beach.

She wanted to be alone.

There she spotted

a broken music box.

Tink quickly got to work.

Her friends watched.

"You fixed it!" Silvermist cried.

They were all amazed
at her tinkering talent.

Tinker Bell enjoyed tinkering.

But she still wanted to go
to the mainland.

As her last hope,

Tink went to Vidia for help.

But Vidia was still angry

with her.

Vidia got an evil idea.

She said Tink should capture

the Sprinting Thistles

to prove she was a garden fairy.

It was a dangerous job.

But Tink had to try.

It was her last chance.

She made a corral and a lasso

to capture the Thistles.

She saddled up

Cheese the mouse and

was on her way.

"It's working!" cried Tink.

Thistles went into the corral!

But then Vidia blew

a strong gust of wind.

The corral gate flew open.

The Thistles ran out.

Hundreds of other Thistles
ran by, too.
Tinker Bell lost control of them.
The Thistles ran this way
and that way through
Springtime Square.
They destroyed all
the springtime supplies.

Everyone was upset.

Spring would have to be canceled.

It was all Tinker Bell's fault.

She flew away in shame.

Tinker Bell decided to leave
Pixie Hollow for good.
She stopped one last time
at the tinkers' workshop.
As she looked around,
she got an idea.
She knew how to save spring!

Back at Springtime Square,
Vidia was punished for
helping the Thistles escape.
And everyone was sad that
spring wouldn't be coming.
"Wait!" Tinker Bell cried.
"I know how we can
fix everything!
But I can't do it alone."

The fairies were eager to help.

Tink showed everyone

what to do.

In the blink of an eye,

Tink's creations filled buckets

with berry paint and seeds.

Soon everything

was ready for spring.

"You did it!"

exclaimed Queen Clarion.

"You saved spring!"

"We *all* did it,"

said Tinker Bell.

Fairy Mary told Tink
she could go to
the mainland, too.
The music box Tink had fixed
belonged to a special little girl.
And only Tinker Bell could
deliver it to her.

Tinker Bell was happy.

Her tinkerings had saved spring.

She was a tinker fairy—

and proud of it!